CATCH that BAT!

Also by Adam Frost

Stop! There's a Snake in Your Suitcase!
Run! The Elephant Weighs a Ton!

More animal adventures with the
Nightingale family coming soon!

CATCH that BAT!

Adam Frost

Illustrated by
Mark Chambers

BLOOMSBURY
LONDON NEW DELHI NEW YORK SYDNEY

*All of the animal facts in this story are true.
Everything else is fiction. Any connection
to any events that have taken place in London
Zoo is purely coincidental.*

Bloomsbury Publishing, London, New Delhi, New York and Sydney

First published in Great Britain in April 2013 by Bloomsbury Publishing Plc
50 Bedford Square, London WC1B 3DP

Manufactured and supplied under licence from the Zoological Society of London

Text copyright © Adam Frost 2013
Illustrations copyright © Mark Chambers 2013

The moral rights of the author and illustrator have been asserted

All rights reserved
No part of this publication may be reproduced or
transmitted by any means, electronic, mechanical, photocopying
or otherwise, without the prior permission of the publisher

A CIP catalogue record for this book is available from the British Library

ISBN 978 1 4088 2708 6

Typeset by Hewer Text UK Ltd, Edinburgh
Printed and bound in Great Britain by CPI Group (UK) Ltd, Croydon CR0 4YY

1 3 5 7 9 10 8 6 4 2

www.storiesfromthezoo.com
www.bloomsbury.com
www.adam-frost.com

To Erin and Alice,
whose dad knows a lot about bats

Chapter 1

Tom and Sophie Nightingale were on their way back from the cinema with their grandad. They had all been to see *AstroKid v The Man-Eating Martians* in 3D and were talking about the amazing special effects. They had just stepped on to the towpath that led down to the marina where they all lived, when every light in the area went out.

The lamp posts along the canal flickered and died, the houseboats in the marina were thrown into darkness and the houses along the edge of Regent's Park were suddenly swallowed up by the night.

'It's the man-eating Martians!' exclaimed Tom. 'They must be here!'

'Don't be daft, Tom,' replied his big sister, Sophie. 'It's just a power cut.'

'So what do we do now?' Tom wailed. 'How are we going to fight the Martians when we can't even see them?'

'It'll be OK, Tom,' Grandad replied, clapping Tom on the back and making him jump. 'We just have to use our other senses, that's all.'

'What do you mean, "our other senses"?' Tom asked.

'Our sense of hearing, our sense of touch,' said Grandad. 'Millions of creatures wake up at night. Bats, owls, hedgehogs, badgers . . . and they get around just fine.'

'How's hearing going to help?' Tom asked. 'I can't hear anything.'

'Course you can,' said Grandad. 'Just listen.' He tapped on the path with his walking stick. 'Hear that?'

'It sounds like concrete,' said Tom.

'Exactly. So we know we're on the path. You try.'

He reached for Tom's arm in the darkness and placed his walking stick in his grandson's hand.

Tom began to tap the path and move slowly forward.

After a few seconds, he exclaimed, 'I can do it!'

At the same time, Sophie said, 'My eyes are beginning to adjust. I think I can see our barge.' She reached out with one arm. 'Yes, I can feel the railings by our section of the towpath.'

'That's the idea,' Grandad said. He took a deep breath. 'And I can smell the ivy that grows along the bank.'

They all moved towards the side of the marina where the houseboats were moored.

Tom and Sophie lived with their parents on

a barge called the *Jessica Rose* but generally known as *The Ark*. If it hadn't been for the power cut, it would have been possible to see all the animals painted on the sides of the boat. The surrounding water had been worked into the design too, so there were hippos wallowing in it, penguins diving into it, elephants drinking from it and flamingos wading in it.

A few metres further along from *The Ark*, the next dark shape was Grandad's houseboat, the *Molly Magee*.

Tom gave Grandad his walking stick back and said, 'I think I can do this last bit.' Then he felt for the edge of *The Ark* with his foot and launched himself into the air.

'Tom!' Sophie exclaimed.

'What?' replied the voice of Tom in the darkness. 'It's fine. I'm totally used to the dark now. Come on – the door's down here.'

At that moment, the edge of the houseboat door glowed and opened. Mrs Nightingale was standing there, holding a candle.

'Hello, you three,' she said.

Tom and Sophie walked carefully down the steps.

'I'm going to check on my place,' said Grandad. 'See you in a bit.'

'Bye, Grandad,' said Tom.

'Thanks for taking us to the cinema,' added Sophie.

As Tom and Sophie entered the living room, Rex, the family terrier, ran up to greet them, sniffing and snuffling at Tom's shoes and trousers.

Sophie gave Rex a quick pat and then hurried to check on her ferret and her rats. She returned after a few seconds with a rat on her shoulder. 'They're all fine, especially Eric. I think rats must quite like the dark.'

In the meantime, Mrs Nightingale was

rummaging in the cupboard under the sink, looking for more candles.

'Where's Dad?' Tom asked.

'Your father is out on the bank, trying to get our emergency generator to work.' She emerged from the cupboard with a pair of candles and a box of matches. 'Last time he went near it, it caught fire twice and burnt off one of his eyebrows.'

'Oh, OK,' said Tom. 'What are those?'

He was pointing at a helmet with a pair of binoculars strapped to it.

'They're night vision goggles,' Mrs Nightingale said. 'I found them at the back of our wardrobe. I thought they might help your father fix the generator but naturally he left them behind.'

'Brilliant!' exclaimed Tom. He grabbed the helmet and slid it on to his head, fiddling with the chinstrap.

'You'd better not break them before I've had a go,' Sophie said.

Tom was squinting through the binoculars.

'You can see everything!' he exclaimed. 'And it turns everyone into a Martian. Rex and Eric have gone bright green. But, you know, that's kind of cool as well.'

He swung around, narrowly avoiding whacking Sophie with the binoculars.

'Mum, Grandad was talking about animals that wake up at night,' Tom said. 'Is this how they see?'

'In some cases,' said Mrs Nightingale. 'What happens is, those goggles magnify all the available light. There's infrared light coming from the other side of the canal out there, but it's too dim for us to see just with our eyes. But when you put those goggles on, they take all those tiny points of light and make them much, much brighter.'

'So that's what nocturnal animals do?' Tom asked.

'Some of them,' said Mrs Nightingale. 'Take owls, for instance. Their eyes are huge – they take up most of their skull. In fact, their eyes are so big that they can't even move them. That's why they have to twist their heads around.'

'Wow,' said Tom.

'In those huge eyes,' Mrs Nightingale went on, 'they have these amazing cells that can pick up the tiniest dots of light. We have them too, but they have ten times as many – which means they can see a hundred times better than us at night.'

'Wow,' said Tom again. 'And is everything green for them as well?'

'No, that's just those goggles,' said his mum with a smile.

'It must be my turn now,' complained Sophie.

Mrs Nightingale nodded. 'Give them to your sister, Tom.'

Tom groaned and took the helmet off.

Sophie handed Eric to her mother and fastened

the helmet chinstrap. Mrs Nightingale returned the rat to his cage and then came back to the living room.

Tom had been thinking.

'I wish I was a nocturnal animal,' he said.

'Hang on,' Mrs Nightingale said. 'Not all nocturnal animals have adapted like owls. Think about bats or moles. Their vision has got worse, not better. Mind you, their other senses have developed to compensate.'

'Oh yeah, Grandad said that,' Tom said.

'Moles are my favourite,' Mrs Nightingale said. 'They have an amazing sense of touch. They can sense the tiniest vibration in the soil around them.'

'Cool,' said Tom. 'Being a human is rubbish at night-time, that's for sure.'

'Mum, look, over there!' Sophie said, pointing at the window and squinting through the goggles at the other side of the canal.

'We can't see anything, can we?' Tom said, rolling his eyes.

Sophie pulled off the helmet and handed it to her mother.

'Something's fallen in the canal and it can't get out,' Sophie said. 'It looks like a puppy.'

Mrs Nightingale looked through the binoculars. She saw a small mammal, scrabbling at the sides of the canal, desperate to find a foothold in the brickwork.

'It's a young fox,' said Mrs Nightingale. 'It must have misjudged a jump. Foxes are good swimmers, but it looks like this one's struggling.'

'We've got to help it,' said Sophie.

'Sometimes it's best not to interfere with nature, Sophie,' said Mrs Nightingale.

'But that's your job, isn't it?' Sophie protested. 'Vets interfere with nature all the time.'

'Hmm,' said Mrs Nightingale. 'You do have a point.'

'Cool, let's go,' said Tom. 'It's got to be better than staying here in the pitch black waiting for the telly to work. Besides, we practised moving around in the dark with Grandad and I was brilliant at it.'

Sophie had already put her coat on and was standing by the door. Mrs Nightingale blew out the candles on the table. She took a pair of torches out of a kitchen drawer and put one in her pocket. She gave the other to Sophie.

Tom had picked up the night vision goggles and was strapping them on.

'What are you doing, Tom?' Mrs Nightingale asked.

'They'll help us to see the fox,' said Tom.

Mrs Nightingale thought for a moment. 'Well, those goggles belong to the zoo, so you have to be very careful.'

'Course,' said Tom, and walked out of the door, banging the top of the helmet on the frame and knocking a pot plant off a window ledge with the binoculars.

Mrs Nightingale picked up the pieces with a sigh and ordered Rex into his basket.

Then the three of them stepped on to the towpath.

Chapter 2

Tom, Sophie and Mrs Nightingale stood next to their houseboat getting their bearings. There was no light coming from anywhere except the torches that Sophie and Mrs Nightingale were holding.

'Let's tell your father what we're doing,' Mrs Nightingale said.

Tom squinted through the night vision goggles and peered along the bank.

'I can't see him,' he said. 'I thought you said he was fiddling with the generator.'

Then they heard someone humming. The sound was coming from further along the towpath. They found their father next to one of the marina's power points, slotting a plug into one of the spare sockets.

There was a small explosion and a puff of black smoke floated past Mr Nightingale's face.

'That's the third time it's done that,' he said.

Mrs Nightingale told him what they were doing.

'Excellent,' he said. 'It should all be fixed when you get back.'

Sophie was tugging at her mum's sleeve. 'Come on, we don't have much time.'

Tom, Sophie and Mrs Nightingale crossed over the bridge to the other side of the canal. Mrs Nightingale and Sophie were flashing their torches on the water.

Tom adjusted the lenses on the night vision goggles and saw the fox's head through the binoculars, bobbing up and down in the water.

'It's still alive,' he said.

Mrs Nightingale shone her torch into the undergrowth. 'Let's look for a branch or plank. Then it can climb up on to the bank.'

Sophie and Mrs Nightingale walked up the verge of the towpath, crunching through the grass and twigs.

'It's swimming the other way,' Tom whispered, 'I think it's scared.'

Mrs Nightingale and Sophie tried to search more quietly, but it was no use – they kept making snapping and cracking noises.

'It's heading down the canal,' said Tom, twisting the end of the binoculars to zoom in on the fox's location.

The three of them began to walk quickly and quietly along the towpath, following the fox as it swam towards Camden.

'It's going to end up at the lock,' Sophie whispered, 'and then what will it do?'

They crossed back over the bridge.

'I've lost it,' Tom said.

'Give me that helmet,' Sophie hissed.

'No, there it is,' Tom said, pointing at a fork in the canal.

Sophie shone her torch on to the water and picked out a small sleek head.

'It doesn't know what it's doing any more,' said Mrs Nightingale. 'It's exhausted.'

'Mum, can it see us? Does it have eyesight like an owl?' Tom asked.

'No, no,' Mrs Nightingale said. 'A fox's vision is pretty average. It's all about hearing.'

'Then we've got to stop chasing it,' said

Tom. 'It probably thinks we're trying to eat it. All it can hear is Sophie clumping around in the dark.'

'I do NOT clump!' Sophie said.

'We should imagine we're the fox,' Tom said, 'If you were him, what would it take to get you out of the water?'

Sophie thought for a moment. 'It needs to hear something reassuring,' she said.

'Hey,' said Tom, 'remember when we were walking down the towpath and we heard Dad humming?'

'Yes,' said Sophie, nodding slowly. 'It told us it was him.'

'Hmm, yes,' Mrs Nightingale chipped in. 'People often sing in the dark to let others know that they are there. They sometimes don't even know they're doing it.'

'So we need to make fox noises,' said Tom, 'so he knows we're friendly.'

'OK, but what do foxes sound like?' Sophie asked.

'That's easy,' said Mrs Nightingale, and she started making a sound like a dog barking.

Then she thought for a moment. 'Actually, that probably sounds like an older fox warning him off. A mother greeting her kit would be more like this.' She made a low huffing noise, like an old lady getting out of breath.

Tom and Sophie copied her.

After a minute or so, they stopped to get their breath back.

Mrs Nightingale shone her torch on the canal. Tom looked through his goggles.

'It's sort of treading water,' said Tom.

They starting huffing and grunting again.

'It's no use,' said Tom. 'It's not moving any closer. And it looks like it's getting tired.'

'Let's try appealing to its sense of smell,' said Mrs Nightingale. 'That's pretty powerful too.'

'Well, what do foxes eat, Mum?' Sophie asked. 'I thought it was anything and everything.'

'It is,' said Mrs Nightingale, 'but they do have favourite things.'

'Like what?' asked Tom.

'Small rodents,' said Mrs Nightingale. 'Mice and rats.'

'Rats!' exclaimed Tom. 'Well, we're all right then.'

'What do you mean?' asked Mrs Nightingale.

'Well, Sophie's got rats, hasn't she,' Tom said.

'Hang on, what are you saying?' Sophie asked.

'Yes, I suppose their smell would attract him,' Mrs Nightingale agreed.

'Wait a minute!' Sophie exclaimed. 'We are NOT using Eric and Ernie as BAIT.'

'I'm not suggesting the fox actually scoffs them,' Tom said.

'Well, what are you saying then?' Sophie said, with her hands on her hips.

'I dunno,' said Tom. 'Maybe you could put them in the cat's travel bag. They'd be safe and have lots of space.'

'They'd probably quite like being out at night-time,' said Mrs Nightingale. 'Rats are nocturnal too. But it's up to you, Sophie.'

Tom was looking at the water. 'It's hardly moving now. Look, you'd better decide fast. Come on, it was you that wanted to rescue it in the first place.'

'Give me those,' Sophie said.

She clipped on the goggles and watched the fox paddling weakly. She tried making the gruff barking noise again. The fox didn't seem to notice.

'OK, fine,' said Sophie.

She ran off along the towpath.

'Bring other food too,' her mother called out. 'Jam, Marmite, anything you find in the cupboard.'

'OK!' Sophie shouted back.

'Is the Marmite for us?' Tom asked. 'All this saving animals is making me hungry.'

Mrs Nightingale kept her torch trained on Sophie's outline on the opposite bank. She knew that Sophie would be perfectly safe in the marina, but still felt better when she could see her.

A couple of minutes later, Sophie was back.

In her left hand, she held Eric and Ernie in a large carry case with a metal grille at the front. In her right, she was carrying a plastic bag full of chinking glass jars, tins and plastic tubs.

'OK,' said Mrs Nightingale, 'let's stand at the top of that slope over there. If the fox gets to that point, it should be able to climb out.'

They positioned themselves next to a dip in the towpath that kayakers used to drop their boats into the canal.

Sophie put the rats down at her feet. Mrs Nightingale opened a jam jar and a tub of Marmite.

'OK, he should find those smells pretty interesting,' she said.

Tom was peering through the goggles.

'It's definitely sniffing the air,' he said.

Eric and Ernie were making excited squeaking noises.

Tom fiddled with the goggles and zoomed right in on the fox's face.

'It looks curious,' he said, 'but I don't think it's moving.'

Mrs Nightingale started making the gruff mother-fox noise. Sophie and Tom joined in.

The fox continued to sniff the air and look interested.

'It must be able to smell us too,' said Mrs Nightingale.

'Do we need to hide?' Tom asked.

'I'm not leaving Eric and Ernie out here on their own,' said Sophie.

'I saw this film about gamekeepers in Africa,' said Tom. 'They can get really close to the lions and zebras by removing their human smell.'

'Hmm,' said Mrs Nightingale. 'That can work.'

'Come on then,' said Tom. He put his hand in the jar nearest to him and started rubbing jam on his cheeks.

'Er . . . no way,' said Sophie.

Tom put his other hand in the tub of Marmite and smeared it on his hands.

Then he looked through his goggles at the fox.

'It's starting to paddle this way!' he announced.

Mrs Nightingale sighed. 'I suppose it will all come out in the wash,' she said. She wiped Marmite around her neck and dabbed jam on her nose and forehead.

Tom was zooming in again. 'It's definitely working! It's speeding up!' he whispered.

'Wow!' exclaimed Sophie. She pulled open a tin of baked beans and rubbed them on her hands.

'We should make the fox noises too,' said Tom, 'in case it gets suspicious.'

The three of them made the harsh huffing noise – louder than ever.

At that moment, Mrs Scraggs from the houseboat next to theirs came walking along the towpath with a torch. She glanced at the three Nightingales – crouching down on the path, making strange barking noises, with a travel bag full of rats in front of them and multicoloured food on their faces. 'Hello!' she said cheerily, as if nothing unusual was happening.

The Nightingales kept grunting for another minute or two.

The fox placed one front leg and then the other on the bank of the canal. Then it pulled itself out, the water rushing off its fur and sloshing around its feet.

Tom and Sophie wanted to shout, 'Hooray!' – but knew it would scare the fox off.

Weak and trembling from the ordeal, the

young fox tottered
across the towpath,
snout in the
air.

'Here you
are,' whispered Sophie,
and nudged the pot of Marmite. The fox lowered
his head and ate ravenously from the tub.

When it had finished, it looked up at the three
strange faces covered in gunk and gloop that
were looking back at him. Mrs Nightingale
made a low growling noise and the fox cocked
its head and gave her an odd look.

Then it seemed to make up its mind. It trot-
ted off along the towpath and vanished into a
bramble patch.

Tom and Sophie looked at each other. Now
there was no reason to hold back. 'Hooray!
Hooray!' they both shouted, hugging each other
and jumping up and down.

Then they heard a buzzing sound from the
lamp post next to them. It flickered on, as did

all the other lights and lamp posts in the marina.

'Oh,' said Tom, sounding disappointed. 'It was way better when everything was dark.'

'That was rather fun, wasn't it?' Mrs Nightingale agreed.

'Mum, why *are* some animals nocturnal?' asked Sophie, as the three of them started to walk back along the canal.

'Well, usually because that's when their food is awake. Bats eat flying insects like mosquitoes and moths. And night is when mosquitoes and moths wake up. Owls eat mice and rats – and most rodents in England wake up in the evening.'

'Oh dear,' said Sophie, looking down at Eric and Ernie. 'It sounds like everyone wants to eat you.'

Eric and Ernie were sticking their noses through the metal grille of the travel bag, sniffing at the food on Sophie's hands.

'Tom,' Mrs Nightingale said, 'could you not lick jam off your hands?'

'I'm not,' Tom insisted. Then he said, 'I'm licking Marmite off my hands.'

Mrs Nightingale rolled her eyes. 'You can have a snack when we get back.'

Tom smiled.

'AFTER you've had a bath,' she added.

Tom groaned.

Chapter 3

Two days later, it was the weekend. Mr and Mrs Nightingale had to go to work and, as always, Tom and Sophie went along.

'Can we go out again tonight?' Tom asked his mum as they walked through the zoo gates. 'I want to see more nocturnal animals.'

'Well, why don't you have a look at the zoo's nocturnal animals first?' Mrs Nightingale suggested.

'Good one, Mum,' said Tom, 'but they'll all be asleep, won't they?'

'Not in the Nightzone, they won't,' said Mrs Nightingale. 'They turn all the lights off during

the day so the animals are active. You'll see armadillos, scorpions, giant jumping rats, all sorts.'

'I forgot about the Nightzone,' said Tom.
'Come on, Soph. Let's spend all day in there.
And all night!'

'Well, there's no point being there at night,'
said Mrs Nightingale. 'That's when they turn
the lights ON. So the animals can get some
sleep.'

'Oh. Right,' said Tom.

'Look, ask for Terry when you get inside,' Mrs
Nightingale said. 'He'll tell you everything.'

Tom and Sophie said goodbye to their parents
and walked past the African hunting dogs. They
reached the big glass entrance doors that led to
the Nightzone and the Rainforest Lookout.
They went downstairs and walked through a set
of doors into a long dark tunnel. Apart from tiny
strip lights on the floor, everything else was dark.
They turned a corner and were suddenly
surrounded by glass enclosures full of scurrying,
flying, leaping, climbing and burrowing animals.

'Now THAT is weird,' said Tom.

He was pointing at a tiny shrew-like animal with bald wrinkled skin and four gigantic teeth.

'It says here it's a naked mole rat,' said Sophie, glancing at the sign next to the enclosure. 'It lives underground like a mole, but it doesn't have any claws. So it digs all its tunnels with its teeth.'

Tom looked again at the naked mole rat's face.

'It also says its teeth are OUTSIDE its mouth,' said Sophie, 'not INSIDE like ours. That stops it from swallowing dirt when it's digging.'

'That's amazing,' Tom said, looking closely at the glass case.

'They can dig tunnels that are up to four kilometres long,' concluded Sophie.

'Four kilometres!' exclaimed Tom. 'But he's

only about ten centimetres long! I'm 130 centimetres. So that's like me digging a tunnel that's,
er, fifty-two kilometres! With my teeth!'

Tom spread his mouth wide and bared his
teeth at his sister.

Sophie ignored him and then bounded over
to another glass case.

'An armadillo!' she cried. 'Armadillos are
brilliant!'

Tom joined her and they
watched the arma-
dillo snuffling
and digging at
the floor of its
enclosure, the
armour on its back
opening and closing as it moved.

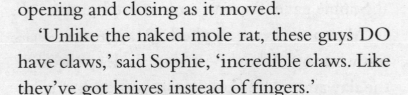

'Unlike the naked mole rat, these guys DO
have claws,' said Sophie, 'incredible claws. Like
they've got knives instead of fingers.'

Tom looked at his hand and said, 'That would
stop you picking your nose.'

'It's also the only mammal with a shell,' said Sophie. 'Look at that armour. It can roll into a ball and nothing can get inside.'

At that moment, they heard a voice behind them.

'You must be Tom and Sophie.'

They turned around and saw a man in his late thirties, with blue eyes and sandy-coloured hair. 'Sounds like you know more about nocturnal animals than I do!'

Sophie blushed.

'I'm Terry,' he said, 'your mum and dad said you want to know more about the Nightzone.'

'Definitely!' said Tom. 'We rescued a fox the other night. We're basically nocturnal ourselves.'

Sophie gave Tom an embarrassed nudge.

'Me too!' Terry replied. 'Daytime is seriously boring. All the best animals sleep through the day and wake up when it gets dark. Lions, tigers, leopards, possums, wombats, raccoons, koalas, coyotes, badgers, hedgehogs . . . the list goes on and on. Let me show you some more.'

'Cool!' said Tom.

'Thanks,' said Sophie.

Terry led them both over to a glass enclosure with two large black creepy-crawlies inside.

'Let's start with one of the smallest,' said Terry. 'The emperor scorpion!'

Tom and Sophie pressed their faces against the glass.

'Nocturnal animals are some of the most successful on the planet,' said Terry. 'Scorpions have been around for 300 million years. They saw the dinosaurs come and go. And you know what? They looked exactly the same then as they do now. They haven't needed to change or evolve because they're perfect the way they are.'

'Wow,' said Tom. 'You mean they've always been good at everything?'

'Exactly,' said Terry, 'they've got large claws to catch their food. And if their food struggles, look at that stinger at the end of their tail. They jab with that and their prey is paralysed. Plus if anything catches them, that armour on their back is tough as nails. Literally. It's got iron and zinc in it. They can be frozen solid, they can eat nothing for a year, they can be held underwater for three days, and they still wouldn't be dead. They can survive a nuclear-bomb blast. In fact, the most likely cause of death for a scorpion is . . .'

'Er . . .' stammered Tom. 'Zombies? Vampires?'

Sophie sighed. 'Another scorpion?' she suggested.

'Exactly,' said Terry with a grin. 'And best of all, they have adapted perfectly to life at night.'

'How?' asked Tom.

'Can you see their eyes?' Terry asked. 'They've got eight of them. That means they can see incredibly well, even when it's dark. They can also see 360 degrees – quite handy when something's creeping up on you. And, most amazingly of all, they've got a pigment in their eyes that kicks in when the sun comes out. It makes their eyes ten thousand times less light sensitive.'

'That IS clever,' Sophie said.

'Yep,' said Terry. 'It's like they've got built-in sunglasses. And watch this.'

He pressed a button next to the case. A purple light came on and the two scorpions glowed white.

'Their shells are sensitive to ultraviolet light,' said Terry. 'Now, WE can't see ultraviolet light, but they can. Which means they can see each other. Even when it's a moonless desert night.'

'Insects aren't exactly my favourite things,' said Sophie, 'but that is pretty impressive.'

'Insects aren't my favourite things either,' said Terry, 'but scorpions are arachnids. They've got eight legs. Like spiders.'

'Oh,' said Sophie.

Tom couldn't help smiling. He couldn't remember the last time his sister had got anything wrong, particularly about animals.

Terry showed them all the other animals in the Nightzone and explained how they'd adapted to life in the dark.

There was a loris, with gigantic eyes that could see insects even when it was pitch black, and cave crickets, with gigantic antennae that helped them to feel their way through dark, murky crevices.

'And here's the most famous of all nocturnal animals!' announced Terry.

He was standing in front of a wide glass case that was full of small brown bats.

'These are Seba's Short–tailed Bats,' said Terry. 'They're originally from South America.'

'There are so many of them in there,' said Tom.

'Well, bats are used to living in large colonies,' said Terry. 'Take Bracken Cave in Texas, for example. Twenty million bats live in it. Can you imagine? One cave – twenty million bats.'

'I wouldn't want to wander in there by mistake,' said Tom.

'I know,' said Terry. 'No other mammal in the world lives in such large huddled groups. In fact, there are lots of things that bats do that other mammals don't. Largely because they're nocturnal.'

'Like what?' Tom asked.

'Tom!' Sophie exclaimed. 'Look at them!'

'I am looking at them,' said Tom. 'It's dark in there, OK?'

'Haven't you noticed they're *flying*?' Sophie said.

Terry chuckled. 'That's right, Sophie. There are thousands and thousands of types of mammals in the world. From dogs to dolphins, from wallabies to whales. But bats are the only mammals that can fly.'

'Wow,' Tom said, staring through the glass. 'How come though?'

'Well, if they couldn't fly,' explained Terry, 'they wouldn't be able to reach their food. Flying insects like mosquitoes and moths. Fruit hanging on high branches.'

'So do they just flap their wings like birds?' Sophie asked.

'No, they sort of rotate them,' said Terry, 'like they're doing the breaststroke in mid-air.'

'And how come we can't fly?' Tom asked, looking at his arms and flapping them tentatively.

Terry smiled. 'You'd need to be a very different shape. Bats' wings have the same basic structure as your hand. Only the fingers have got longer and longer. And the skin between the fingers has got wider and wider. And the finger bones have got lighter and lighter. Until eventually the hand has turned into a wing. If you were a bat, each of your fingers would need to be half a metre long – as long as your legs!'

'They'd just drag on the floor,' said Sophie, looking at her fingers.

'Who cares though?!' Tom exclaimed. 'You could fly! You'd never be *on* the floor!'

There was a crackly noise and Terry looked down at the walkie-talkie on his belt. He picked it up and said: 'Hello, Nightzone.' The crackling continued for a few seconds and then Terry said, 'On my way.'

He clipped the walkie-talkie back on to his belt. 'I'm needed over at the fruit bat enclosure. Want to come?' he said.

'Yes!' Tom and Sophie both exclaimed.

'Where are they though?' Tom asked. 'Aren't they here with the other nocturnal animals?'

'They've got a section all to themselves,' Terry explained. 'They're quite big so they need more space.'

Terry set off towards the exit, followed by Tom and Sophie.

'How big is big?' Tom asked.

'They have a wingspan of just under a metre,' said Terry.

'Is that pretty big for a bat?' Sophie asked.

'About in the middle,' said Terry. 'The world's smallest is the bumblebee bat – it's smaller than a jellybean. The biggest is the Bismarck flying fox. It has a wingspan of almost two metres. That's about the same as a man holding his arms out.'

Terry held his arms out and pretended to glide along.

Tom copied him, rotating his arms as if he was doing the breaststroke.

Sophie shook her head and looked embarrassed. Then, when she realised that nobody was looking, she joined in.

Chapter 4

Tom, Sophie and Terry walked around the back of the Rainforest Lookout, glancing up at the lemurs. Terry ducked into a door underneath their enclosure and Tom and Sophie followed.

'I didn't even realise this was here,' Sophie said.

They were in a long, dark corridor, looking into a dimly lit enclosure. Behind the glass dozens of large brown bats were flitting from side to side.

'They look totally different from the ones we just saw,' said Tom. 'These don't really look like bats at all.'

'Ah, that's because when you think of bats, you think of microbats,' said Terry. 'These are megabats.'

'Megabats?' said Tom. 'Why haven't I heard of megabats? They sound awesome. If I was a bat, I'd definitely be a megabat.'

'I think microbats sound cooler,' said Sophie. 'They sound like they're tiny robots. Full of microchips.'

'Actually, that's true,' admitted Tom. 'Can you be a microbat AND a megabat?'

Terry shook his head. 'One or the other. Microbats are the ones we get in the UK. Small scrunched-up faces. Stubby noses. Big ears. Tend to eat insects. Megabats look more like squirrels or foxes with wings. That's why sometimes they're called flying foxes. They tend to eat fruit. And they're generally a lot, lot bigger.'

'Then I'll go back to being a megabat,' said Tom.

He stared at the fruit bats in the enclosure. A keeper was placing some pears and berries on a feeding station and the bats were swooping across, ready to tuck in. The keeper was wearing sturdy-looking black gloves.

'OK, I just need to observe Polly,' said Terry.

'Is she the keeper?' Sophie asked.

'No, Polly's the bat over there on her own,' said Terry. 'She was off her food yesterday, so I need to see if she's any better today.'

Tom and Sophie watched Polly and then watched Terry watching Polly.

'She's sniffing the air,' said Terry, 'looking awake. She wasn't even doing that yesterday. Let's see if she joins the others for some lunch. If she does, we can stop worrying.'

'You mean – you're worried now? How come?' Sophie asked.

'We're continually worried about these bats,' said Terry. 'You see, they're Rodrigues Fruit Bats. From Mauritius, near India. And they're critically endangered – only a couple of hundred are left in the wild.'

'A couple of hundred? That's all?' Sophie said.

'I know,' said Terry. 'I sometimes wonder what that must feel like. Imagine if there were only two hundred human beings left on the whole planet. It'd be pretty lonely, eh?'

Tom and Sophie thought about this and nodded.

'And knowing my luck,' added Tom, 'it would just be me and 199 girls. Or me and 199 *teachers*.'

'I don't think it works like that,' said Sophie.

'It flippin' would for me,' said Tom.

'A lot of their natural habitat has gone,' said Terry, gazing at the enclosure, 'and global warming isn't helping either. It's lucky we got involved when we did. Hopefully we can save the species.'

'Maybe being a megabat isn't so good after all,' Tom said.

'Oh, it's still pretty good,' said Terry. 'Though, I have to say, if I could choose, I'd probably be a microbat.'

'How come?' Sophie asked.

'Isn't it better to be bigger?' Tom said.

'Maybe,' said Terry, 'but for me the most amazing thing about bats is echolocation. And those bats in there can't echolocate. Hardly any megabats can.'

'I've read about that,' Sophie said. 'It's something to do with finding your way around using squeaks.'

Terry nodded. 'As you know, bats are nocturnal, which means they can't rely on sunlight to help them see. Now, if you're a fruit bat –' he nodded at the bats in the enclosure – 'you'll mainly use your sense of smell to work out where you are. But microbats, like the ones we saw in the Nightzone, are different. They rely on hearing. When they're flying, they make a high-pitched squeaking noise. This noise will bounce off anything in the surrounding area. Maybe a tree trunk. Maybe a moth. The bats' large ears hear the noise bouncing back. From the speed and volume of the echo, they work out where the object is.'

'That's amazing!' said Tom.

'I know,' said Terry, 'but that's not all. Then they squeak again. The noise rebounds again. Now they have two pieces of information. They can work out whether the object is big or small, whether it's moving or standing still. They squeak again and get another update. As they get closer and closer to the object, they squeak more and more, continually getting more data. Then finally they catch the moth or dodge the tree or land in the cave.'

'That's incredible!' said Sophie.

'Exactly,' said Terry. 'Pretty amazing. And think about what they're actually doing. They're putting together a 3D map of the world around them. Using nothing but sound waves. And changing it every millisecond. *While they're moving.*'

Tom and Sophie let this information sink in.

'Looks like we've got a new favourite animal,' Sophie said.

Tom nodded. 'Now I understand why Batman wanted to dress up as a bat. Spiderman and Catwoman got it all wrong.'

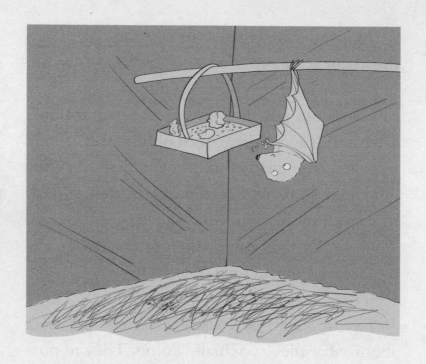

At that moment, Polly the bat sprang off her perch, fluttered across the enclosure and landed on the feeding station. Terry smiled. 'She's OK. All is well,' he said.

He walked towards the exit, with Tom and Sophie following him. As he opened the door to leave, Mrs Nightingale stepped in through it.

'Ah, Terry, glad you're here,' she said. 'We need your help at the hospital.'

She peered over Terry's shoulder.

'Hello, you two,' she said. 'What's your favourite nocturnal animal so far?'

'Well, generally speaking, bats,' said Sophie.

'But we can't decide between these fruit bats and the Seba's Short-tailed Bats,' said Tom. 'There are so many differences between micro-bats and megabats and some of them –'

'OK, OK, I get it,' said Mrs Nightingale. 'You like bats. You can tell me more later. Right now, I need to borrow Terry.'

Terry smiled. 'See you soon, you two. Maybe next weekend?'

'Tomorrow,' Tom and Sophie said in unison.

'Same time, same place,' Sophie added.

Chapter 5

That evening, Tom and Sophie walked back to *The Ark* with their parents. They were talking mostly about bats, but also discussing scorpions, naked mole rats, pottos, lorises and armadillos.

'Can we go out on the canal bank tonight?' Sophie asked her mum.

'Yeah, we want to try to spot more nocturnal animals,' said Tom.

'OK, but you stay inside the marina,' said Mrs Nightingale.

'If you want to do any bat-spotting further along the canal, you come and get one of us,' said Mr Nightingale.

'What do you mean, "bat-spotting"?' Sophie asked.

'Well, I thought you said you were going out looking for nocturnal animals?' Mr Nightingale said.

'Yeah, but we were thinking foxes, badgers and mice,' said Sophie.

'We didn't realise there were any bats on our part of the canal,' said Tom.

'Now you've done it,' sighed Mrs Nightingale.

'So there are real bats — actually living here near our boat?' Sophie asked.

'Loads,' said Mr Nightingale. 'Daubenton's and Common Pipistrelles mainly. But maybe others. They feed on the midges you see hovering above the water, and live in the trees nearby.'

'Great, we can use the night-vision goggles to watch them in action,' said Tom.

'Sorry, Tom,' said Mr Nightingale, 'those goggles actually belonged to the zoo and I had to give them back. Tell you what, if you really want to see some bats, ask your grandad. He's photographed loads of nocturnal animals in his time. He knows all kinds of tricks.'

Tom and Sophie wolfed down their dinner. As they ate, Sophie flicked through *The Junior Bat Spotter's Guide* and Tom skim-read *The Big Book of British Bats.*

They glugged down their water, piled into their coats and ran along the towpath to Grandad's boat.

Grandad listened to them carefully as they rattled through their plan for the evening.

'Excellent idea,' he said. 'Now, there are all kinds of ways of spotting animals at night, but the best thing is to use a specially adapted torch. Come with me.'

He walked along the narrow corridor that ran the length of his houseboat, stopping at a small cupboard door. Then he opened it and beckoned Tom and Sophie to follow him inside.

'What's this, Grandad?' Tom asked. 'A secret portal to another world?'

'Something like that,' Grandad replied.

They found themselves in a small dark room with no windows, and a shelf of strange-looking liquids in plastic bottles. There was a sink in one corner and two washing lines attached to the ceiling. The washing lines had photographs of animals hanging from them.

'This is my darkroom,' Grandad said. I use it to develop my own photos. I use the chemicals you can see in those bottles.'

'I knew you liked taking photos, but this is crazy,' said Tom.

'So why does it need to be dark, Grandad?' Sophie asked.

'Because when you develop photos taken on an old-fashioned camera, it must be totally pitch black,' said Grandad. 'Any light spoils the film and makes the whole photo completely white. Which is why . . .'

Grandad closed the door.

The room was totally dark. There wasn't a hint of light from anywhere.

'Wow,' whispered Sophie.

Tom held his hand in front of his face but couldn't even see the outline.

Then a small lamp came on in the corner of the room. It gave off a faint red glow.

'This is my safe light,' said Grandad. 'It has a special red filter over it. It means I can see what I'm doing, but it stops the light from damaging the film.'

He opened a drawer and took out two torches.

'These torches have the same kind of filter on them. They'll help you to see in the dark.'

He handed one torch to Tom and the other to Sophie.

'But why don't we just use normal torches?' Tom asked.

'Because bats are a bit like the film in my camera,' said Grandad. 'They don't like bright light. If you use normal torches, they'll be frightened away.'

'Cool,' said Tom, flicking his torch on and off.

'Are you coming with us, Grandad?' Sophie asked.

'No, no,' said Grandad, shaking his head. 'Bat-watching is a young man's game. Or a young lady's, of course. But stop by on your way back – I want to hear all about it.'

'OK, Grandad,' said Tom, heading towards the door.

'Thanks,' said Sophie, following Tom out.

As they ran along the canal, Tom and Sophie chatted about their grandad's darkroom.

'Do you think Mum and Dad would get one of those in our houseboat?' Tom asked.

'What for?' Sophie replied. 'None of us are really into photography.'

'No, I mean for us,' Tom said. 'We love nocturnal animals, right? And we're going to be spending a lot of time looking for them, right? So we need to get used to the dark.'

Sophie shrugged. 'Maybe. But I think just being out on the canal is the best training. I can already feel my eyes adjusting.'

Tom said, 'Me too. I can basically see everything.'

He nearly tripped over a paving stone, but quickly recovered his footing as if it hadn't happened.

They had reached a quiet section of the towpath, just on the edge of the marina. They crouched down and shone their torches on to the water and up into the trees behind them.

'If Mum and Dad let me,' Tom whispered,

'I'd like to become properly nocturnal. You know – sleep during the day.'

'Tom,' Sophie said, 'they're not going to let you. What about school?'

'Didn't Dad go to night school?' Tom said. 'I'll just do that instead.'

'Yeah, I suppose,' Sophie said.

A few seconds later, they heard distant fluttering and squeaking. They shone their torches towards the sound.

'I can't believe there are bats right here and we didn't even know about it,' Tom said quietly.

'I know,' Sophie replied. 'We spend so much time in the zoo that we forget about all the animals that live right here.'

'Where are they though?' Tom said. 'I can't pick them out.'

They both shone their torches on to the water and then up into the trees behind them, but they couldn't see any bats.

There was another series of squeaks.

'Over there by the bridge,' said Sophie.

They could see dark black shapes swooping through the air about fifty metres ahead of them. It wasn't pitch black yet, so the bats were still visible against the deep blue of the evening sky.

'They look like birds from here,' said Tom.

'Let's get closer,' said Sophie.

They walked further along the towpath, keeping the red light of their torches trained on the cloud of bats.

'They must be feeding on the midges that gather under the bridge,' said Sophie.

'Look at that one,' whispered Tom.

He pointed at a bat that was heading in their direction. It was darting up and down, and then hovering in mid-air.

'It must be hunting a moth,' said Sophie.

'So why can't it just catch the moth and eat it?' Tom asked.

'According to that book I was reading, some moths have evolved a defence mechanism,' said Sophie. 'They emit a high-pitched sound that confuses bats. Messes with their echolocation.'

'So what happens?' Tom asked.

'Let's watch. Maybe we'll find out,' Sophie said.

The bat was still hovering in mid-air. Tom and Sophie trained their torches on the bat and saw a moth fluttering just in front of it. The bat jerked upward, the moth flapped backwards, the bat darted forward, the moth fluttered sideways, the bat flew in a clockwise circle, the moth flew in an anticlockwise circle. All of this happened in a split second.

'Wow,' whispered Tom.

The bat suddenly jutted its legs out and swooped forward.

'He caught it,' said Sophie.

The bat darted off, crunching the moth in his jaws.

'So the bat won that one,' Tom said. 'Whoa, look at those ones over there.' He swept his torch back across to the group of bats by the bridge.

'It's like they're dive-bombing,' he said.

Two or three of the bats were flying above the water, getting lower and lower, until finally they skimmed the surface of the canal and took off again.

'I bet they're catching all those insects that hover just above the water,' said Sophie.

'But how come the bats never land in the canal?'

'Maybe their squeaks bounce off the water,' said Sophie, 'so they know when to take off again.'

They shone their torches on a bat that was starting to swoop down towards the water, following it with their beams.

As it skimmed across the surface of the canal, it seemed to catch one insect with its wing and pass it into its mouth, crunching it up with its jaws. But, at the same time, a larger insect disappeared into the bat's tail.

'Did you see that?' Sophie asked.

Tom nodded, puzzled.

Another bat swooped down from the bridge.

It caught a midge with its claws and passed it into its mouth. But a second insect seemed to be scooped up by the bat's tail.

'What do you think it's doing?' Tom asked.

'Keeping some food for later?' Sophie suggested. 'But I can't see how.'

'Let's ask Grandad about it when we get back,' Tom said.

'What are you asking Grandad?' said a voice behind them.

They turned around and saw their grandad standing behind them.

'I've come to round you both up,' he said. 'It's half past eight already.'

'It can't be,' said Sophie. 'We got here at seven.'

'You've been watching bats for an hour and a half,' said Grandad.

'We can't have been,' said Tom. 'That's impossible.'

'Time flies when you're watching bats,' said Grandad with a smile. 'You end up getting drawn into their world. They're great hunters.'

Tom asked Grandad about the bats that had skimmed across the surface of the canal, catching some insects with their wings and seeming to scoop up others with their tails.

'They'll be Daubenton's,' said Grandad, 'very clever bats. They have a pouch under their tails. They can use it to sweep up prey. Also to store anything they catch.'

'So what you're saying is,' Tom said, 'they catch moths with their bottoms.'

'That's it,' said Grandad with a smile.

He led them back along the towpath towards *The Ark*.

'The bats we saw looked like adults,' said Sophie. 'Are there no baby bats around at the moment?'

'Well, they won't be flying anywhere yet,' said Grandad, 'but yes, springtime is usually when bats start having their kits. They wake up from hibernation, the females find a maternity roost and then start having babies shortly afterwards.'

'That's pretty quick, isn't it?' Sophie said.

'Well, one other thing that some bats do is mate before they hibernate,' said Grandad, 'so it's all out of the way. Then they delay getting pregnant while they're hibernating. Everything in their body completely stops. When they wake up, things kick off again and the baby bat starts growing inside its mother.'

'That's amazing,' said Sophie.

'So as well as flying, and echolocating, and

sleeping upside down, they can decide when to have a baby,' said Tom.

Grandad nodded. 'It must be splendid being a bat!'

Chapter 6

All that week at school, neither Tom nor Sophie could concentrate. Tom spent hours drawing pictures of different kinds of bats in the back of his maths book. Sophie nearly got caught secretly reading her *Junior Bat Spotter's Guide* under the table in a history lesson.

Each evening, they couldn't wait for it to get dark so they could go back to the towpath and pick out bats with their torches, whispering about what they could see. By Friday, they had become experts at spotting bats, even at long distances.

'Look at that one!' exclaimed Sophie.

She trained the beam of her torch on a bat that was flapping away from the canal.

'Can you see it?' Sophie said. 'On its back?'

Tom nodded. It was a baby bat, clinging on to its mother's back with its tiny claws.

They watched the mother and baby as they flew off over the trees.

'There's another one,' said Sophie. 'Look.'

Another bat with a small black shape on its back sped across the sky. Then another.

'What do you think they're doing?' Tom asked.

'I don't know,' said Sophie. 'I read in my book that sometimes bats move house. They all decide to leave one roost and find another one. Maybe that's what they're doing.'

Within seconds, the sky above their head was full of squeaking, flapping, fluttering bats. Tom and Sophie shone their torches straight up and stared.

Soon it was quieter again. A few bats were still hovering under the bridge, but there was no sign of the others.

'Will they come back?' Tom asked.

'I don't know,' said Sophie.

'Do you think there are bats in other parts of the marina?' asked Tom.

'Let's find out,' said Sophie.

They turned to leave.

'I know they've gone,' Tom said. 'but it's like I can still hear one of them squeaking.'

'Yeah, I know what you mean,' Sophie said, 'but it's not coming from the sky.'

'So where is it coming from?' Tom asked.

They both listened as hard as they could.

'Let's close our eyes,' said Tom. 'It works for bats.'

They both closed their eyes tight and concentrated on the sounds. The night air was cold on their faces.

They picked out the water lapping the bank in front of them, the trees rustling behind them, the barges creaking further up the canal, the quiet murmur of cars on the street beyond.

'Wow,' said Sophie, her eyes still scrunched up. 'It does actually help.'

'There it is!' exclaimed Tom, holding up his finger. He kept his eyes closed and took a step towards the sound. He stopped and listened again. He took another step.

Seconds later, they were crouching down, looking at a small brown creature squirming in a patch of grass. It was stabbing the ground with its wings, trying to propel itself forward.

'It's a baby bat,' Tom said.

'Maybe it fell off its mum,' said Sophie.

'Do you think she'll come back for it?'

'Not with us here,' said Sophie. 'Come on, we'd better keep an eye on it from a safe distance.'

They waited behind a nearby tree for half an hour, peering out every minute or so. The mother bat did not return.

'It's past eight. We have to go home,' said Tom.

'Five more minutes,' said Sophie.

But still the mother bat didn't come.

'OK, we're taking him with us,' said Sophie.

'Hang on,' said Tom, grabbing her arm. 'Don't you remember the keeper in the fruit bat enclosure. She had special gloves on.'

'What are you saying?' Sophie said.

'I don't think just anyone can pick up a bat,' said Tom.

'I'm not just anyone,' said Sophie, her hands on her hips. 'I know more about animals than anyone else in my year.'

'Go on then,' said Tom, 'pick it up. Get bitten. Accidentally squeeze it to death.'

Sophie hesitated.

'What are you waiting for?' Tom asked, 'Miss "I know more about animals than anyone else ever . . ."'

'OK,' Sophie said, 'give me your phone. I'll ring Grandad.'

'I didn't bring my phone', said Tom. 'I thought you brought your phone.'

Sophie sighed. 'Great, so we both forgot our phones. OK, I'll wait here. You go and fetch Grandad.'

'But I'm not supposed to go anywhere on my own,' Tom said.

'All right,' Sophie said, '*you* stay here and *I'll* go and get Grandad.'

'I'm not supposed to be left anywhere on my own either,' Tom said.

'Argh,' Sophie growled. 'OK, we'll both have to go and get Grandad. Run faster than you've ever run in your life.'

They sped along the towpath and reached Grandad's barge in thirty seconds flat.

Breathlessly they explained what they'd found and that there was no time to lose. Grandad rummaged around in the cupboard under his sink until he found a special pair of gloves and a small cardboard box.

'You did well to come and get me,' Grandad

said. 'Bats need special handling. They're a protected species, after all.'

After what felt like ages to Tom and Sophie, Grandad stood up and said, 'I'm ready. Let's go.'

'He'll still be alive, won't he?' Tom whispered to Sophie.

Then both of them heard a sound: the strange, coughing, growling noise that they'd made last week when they were rescuing the baby fox.

'You don't think that fox we saved would . . . eat . . .' Tom stammered.

'Faster!' gasped Sophie.

They reached the spot where the bat had been found. Tom and Sophie realised that, in their rush to get Grandad, they'd left their torches on his barge.

'How could I be so stupid?' Sophie exclaimed.

'You were just born that way, Soph, don't worry about it,' Tom said.

Sophie narrowed her eyes at her brother. Then they heard the fox growling again.

'Is it nearby?' Sophie whispered.

Tom closed his eyes. 'I think it's keeping its distance. Because of us,' he said.

'Can you hear the baby bat?' Sophie said, closing her eyes too.

'I can't tell,' said Tom.

'Are you sure it was here?' Grandad asked. 'I can't see anything.'

Then Tom pointed at a bush about a metre away from the towpath.

'In there,' he said.

As he stepped towards it, there was a scuffling noise and they saw a dark fox-like shape disappearing down the towpath.

Grandad bent down. 'I can see the bush all right, but I can't make out a bat,' he said.

'I'll guide you,' Tom said, and he moved his grandad's gloved hands towards the tiny form of the baby bat.

'Gosh!' Grandad exclaimed. 'How did you know where it was?'

'I could hear it,' said Tom.

'Tom has got quite good at hearing in the dark,' Sophie admitted begrudgingly.

'Of course!' exclaimed Grandad. 'Younger children can hear high-pitched noises. Us old people lose that ability. It's very lucky you were here when this one dropped off its mother's back. An adult wouldn't have heard a thing.'

Grandad placed the bat very gently in the cardboard box.

'Right, let's give my old friend Terry a ring,' said Grandad, 'and we can get this fellow sorted out.'

'You know Terry too?' Tom said.

'Of course!' Grandad said. 'I was Chief Vet at London Zoo for thirty years, remember. I gave little Terence his first job – mucking out the hippos.'

As they walked back to Grandad's houseboat, Tom asked, 'How old do you think the bat is?'

'No more than three weeks,' said Grandad.

'So do you think that fox we heard would have eaten it?' Sophie asked.

'Heavens, yes!' Grandad exclaimed. 'And if he hadn't, then an owl would have spotted it. There's no doubt about it, you saved the poor creature's life!'

Tom and Sophie both felt a rush of satisfaction. They smiled at each other as they followed their grandad along the canal.

When they reached his boat, Grandad said, 'Right, I'll leave you two on babysitting duty while I tell everyone what's happened.'

Tom and Sophie heard their grandad talking on the phone to Terry and then to their parents. They peered over the edge of the cardboard box and stared at the bat as it explored its temporary home. It used its wings to drag itself from one corner of the box to another.

'Your mum and dad say you have to be home in half an hour,' said Grandad.

Tom and Sophie didn't hear him. They were still staring at the bat.

'What shall we call it?' Sophie asked.

'How about Zoltan, the Dark Lord of the Skies,' Tom suggested.

'No way,' said Sophie. 'What about Madeleine? Or Eloise?'

'But he might be a boy!' protested Tom.

'Or *she* might be a girl,' Sophie said. 'So it has to be a name that works for both girls and boys.'

'Hmm', said Tom, thinking for a moment. Then he said, 'What about Pat?' Pat the bat. That works either way.'

'I say, I like that!' Grandad said.

Sophie looked down at the bat and then up at Grandad. 'Do you think Pat's hurt? I mean, he *or she* must have fallen a long way.'

'Well, your mother can tell us for sure,' said Grandad, 'but I wouldn't have thought so. The grass would have been quite a soft landing.'

'But why was Pat on his mother's back in the first place?' Tom asked.

'We saw loads of bats flying off together at the same time,' Sophie said. 'Were they moving house?'

Grandad thought about this and then nodded. 'That does make sense. Bats often move from one roost to another. Especially if weather conditions change. And it has been cold and rainy down on the canal this week. You see, those mother bats will want to keep their babies safe and warm.'

'It's hardly safe and warm being dropped on to a towpath, is it?' Tom said.

'Well, most of them manage to cling on,' said Grandad. 'This young fellow was just unlucky, that's all.'

'How come bats are so good at clinging on to stuff?' Tom asked. 'I mean, they sleep upside down, without ever letting go, right?'

'They do,' Grandad said. 'And that, Tom, is another incredible thing about bats. You see, when you fall asleep, all your muscles relax. You go limp. But bats do the opposite. When they go to sleep, they clench their muscles. And then they stay like that all night. Extraordinary.'

The door thumped open behind them and Terry walked in.

'Hello, everyone,' he said. 'I hear my two favourite assistants have been out saving bats.'

He was holding a set of portable scales, a white bag, a plastic bottle, a pair of black gloves and a small yellow plastic box.

He went directly to the cardboard box and looked inside.

'Cute, no?'

Tom and Sophie nodded.

After putting on his gloves, Terry lifted the bat gently out of the box and placed it inside the white bag. Then he took out his scales. Unlike scales that you stood on, these were designed to be held in your hand. They had a large hook on the bottom. Terry put the handles of the bag on to the hook and then read the weight on the scales.

'Normal for her age,' said Terry.

'So she's a girl then,' Sophie asked.

Terry nodded.

'So Pat's short for Patricia,' Tom said.

'Is she OK in there?' Sophie asked, staring at the bag.

Terry nodded. 'Bats are used to living in holes and crevices. She couldn't be happier.'

Terry returned the bat to the box. Then he held out the bottle. 'Who wants a go?'

Tom and Sophie took turns wearing the gloves and feeding the bat milk from the tiny bottle.

'Now she needs dinner,' Terry said.

He opened the plastic box and tilted it towards Tom and Sophie. There were hundreds of squirming maggots inside.

'Mealworms,' said Terry, 'yum.'

Sophie and Tom took turns holding a mealworm with a pair of tweezers and dangling it in front of Pat's face. She would tilt her head back, sniff the worm and then crunch it up in her tiny jaws.

'Right, that's the basics done,' said Terry. 'We'll get your mum to look over her in the morning. Just in case she damaged anything in the fall. Give her milk every couple of hours. Mealworms every three or four. Remember, she's used to feeding at night.'

'Hang on,' Grandad said. 'I'm seventy-nine years old. I need my beauty sleep.'

'We'll do it!' Tom and Sophie exclaimed at the same time.

'Hmm,' Grandad said. 'You might be OK the first night. But after a few nights, you'll be exhausted. You won't be able to stay awake at school.'

He glanced over his shoulder and then looked back. 'I've got a better idea.'

He had a glint in his eye.

'You remember my darkroom?' he said.

Tom and Sophie nodded.

'How about we make our own little Nightzone here?' Grandad suggested. 'We'll reverse day and night for Pat the bat. We'll keep her in the dark-room during the day. And I'll leave her in the kitchen with the light on at night. That way, she'll sleep at night-time. And wake up during the day. Just like us. And we'll be able to look after her.'

'Blimey, that's ingenious,' said Terry. 'I might bring a couple of my bats over too!'

'Really?' Tom said. 'Are they huge? Are they vampire bats? Will they fly around the barge?'

'Just joking, Tom, sorry,' Terry said.

He put the scales, the mealworms and the milk bottle down on the table.

'I'll leave these with you,' he said. 'Well done for finding her.'

He peered into the box again.

'Sweet dreams, Pat.'

Chapter 7

The next day was a Saturday. Tom and Sophie leapt out of bed and rushed across to their grandad's barge. Grandad was already up, whistling a Beatles song and frying eggs.

'She's in the darkroom,' he said, 'ready for her breakfast.'

Tom and Sophie went into the darkroom and turned on the red safe light that Grandad used when he was developing his pictures. This meant that they could see what they were doing, but Pat wouldn't be disturbed by the brightness. The children took turns feeding Pat milk and mealworms.

Half an hour later, Mrs Nightingale arrived. She put on a pair of black gloves and inspected Pat's fur, wings and claws.

'She damaged her left wing very slightly in the fall,' she said. 'We'll rub this cream on it for the next couple of days to speed up the healing.'

Mrs Nightingale placed a blob of cream on the end of her right glove and then rubbed it into Pat's wing.

'Is she in pain?' Sophie asked.

'No, not really. But best to be on the safe side. Those mealworms are building her strength up too,' Mrs Nightingale said.

For the rest of the day, Tom and Sophie continued to sit in the darkroom with Pat, feeding her and changing her bedding.

In the middle of the afternoon, Terry's head appeared around the darkroom door.

'How's she doing?' Terry asked.

'Fine,' Tom and Sophie both said.

Terry looked from Tom to Sophie and said,

'You know, we WILL have to return her to the wild at some point.'

'All right. We know,' Tom said.

'But in a way, that is almost as cool as looking after her,' said Terry.

'What do you mean?' asked Sophie.

'Well, we've got a mission now,' Terry said. 'We've got to try to find Pat's mum.'

'What? So she can just drop Pat on her head again!' huffed Tom, folding his arms.

'Pat's mum didn't mean to drop her,' said Terry. 'She'll be worried.'

'But HOW can we find her mum?' said Sophie. 'I read yesterday that there are over a million bats in the UK.'

'And didn't you say she was on her way to a new roost,' said Tom. 'She could be in Scotland by now.'

'Not likely,' said Terry. 'My bet is they flew off to a temporary roost because of the bad weather last week. It got too damp for them. But they won't be far away. And what's more, they might go back to their original roost now it's drying off.'

'So that narrows it down to a few thousand bats then,' said Sophie.

'It wouldn't be a mission if it was easy,' said Terry.

He beckoned them into the kitchen. Lying open on the kitchen table was a large bag containing a black rectangular box with a digital display, a net, a rolled-up sheet of canvas, a small laptop, three torches, a thermos flask, a plastic stick and a gigantic bar of chocolate.

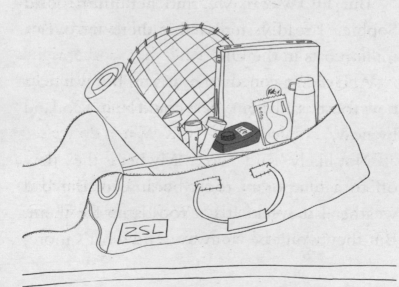

'My bat-finding bag,' announced Terry.

'Do bats like chocolate then?' Tom asked.

'No, the chocolate is for me,' Terry said. 'Finding bats is hungry work. So – are you up for it?'

Sophie glanced back at the darkroom and hesitated.

Tom took the black box out of Terry's bag and said, 'What's this?'

'A bat detector,' said Terry.

'Then I'm definitely up for it!' Tom said, turning the box over in his hands.

Sophie was still looking back at the darkroom. Terry noticed this and said, 'Don't worry, I'm not suggesting we return Pat to her mother right away. Her wing needs to heal first. But it'll help if we know roughly where her home is.'

Sophie nodded firmly. 'OK. When do we set off?'

'Tonight at seven,' Terry said. 'I've cleared it with your mum and dad. We'll start off where you found Pat and work from there.'

And when a brown long-eared bat is resting, his ears are so big that he'll actually put them away. Either he'll roll them up behind his head or tuck them under his wings.'

'That's so cool,' said Sophie, chuckling.

Tom looked impressed, but then his face fell. 'So Pat's mum isn't up there?'

Terry shook his head. 'No, we need to keep looking.'

They walked along the canal and stopped at the next X on Tom's map.

Terry held up the detector. 'Want to try?' he asked.

'Definitely,' Tom said, before Sophie had even opened her mouth.

'OK, turn this dial here slowly until you hear a noise,' Terry said.

'There are definitely bats here,' said Sophie. 'I can hear them without that.'

Tom and Sophie peered up into the dark trees overhead. Tom kept turning the dial on the detector.

'I can't hear anything,' said Terry, 'but the fact that you can means they must be a fairly loud species. Maybe noctules.'

Tom twisted the dial on the detector until it emitted a series of loud pinging noises. He grinned in triumph.

'And there they are,' said Terry. 'Noctules. Oh, I love noctules.'

'It sounds like a laser gun in a science fiction film,' said Tom.

'Or someone twanging a rubber band,' said Sophie.

'Beautiful, aren't they?' said Terry. 'Let me have the detector a minute.'

Tom handed it back and Terry quickly connected it to his laptop. 'Noctules are a big, loud bat. Fast too, about fifty kilometres an hour. And tough – they can survive without food for three or four months if necessary.'

He clicked an icon on his laptop and a series of sound waves rippled across the screen.

'Look, see how the sound waves are getting

closer together,' said Terry, pointing at the screen. 'That means he's increasing the frequency of his call. He's heard an insect. He's hunting.'

The bat detector was making higher and faster noises and the sound waves on the screen were getting closer and closer together.

'What's happening now?' Sophie asked.

'He's closing in,' said Terry.

The sound waves were almost on top of each other. Then they smoothed out and there was a series of sharp clicking noises.

'Now what?' Tom asked.

There was another clicking noise.

'He's eating his dinner,' said Terry.

The sound waves were getting smaller and flattening out.

'And now he's flying out of range,' said Terry.

Tom stared at the screen for a few seconds and then said, 'So what would Pat's mum sound like?'

Terry looked at Tom and smiled. 'Good

question.' He opened a file on his computer and double-clicked it. 'Like this.'

Tom and Sophie heard a rapid fluttering noise. The sound waves on the screen were bunched together very tightly.

'It's like a bird flapping its wings really quickly,' said Sophie.

'Or if you hold a plastic ruler over a desk and flick the end,' said Tom.

'OK,' Sophie said. 'Now we know what we're listening for. On with the mission.'

Terry nodded. He handed the bat detector to Sophie. 'Your turn.'

Sophie smiled and took the detector.

For the next hour, they continued to search up and down the towpath, leaving the marina to hunt along the canal at Camden and Islington. Using the bat detector, they picked up more Common Pipistrelles, long-eared bats and noctules. Behind Regent's Park, they heard a serotine bat, which made a call that was similar to a noctule's but slower and less metallic.

They were having so much fun, they almost forgot about their mission.

Then at half past eight, Terry said, 'OK, I've got to get you two home now.'

'But . . . but . . . we haven't found any Daubenton's yet!' protested Tom.

'And there are loads of places we haven't looked,' added Sophie.

'Look, if I don't get you back at a decent time, your mum will kill me,' Terry said. 'And if she kills me, our mission will be over, won't it?'

'She wouldn't *actually* kill you,' Tom said.

'She's not that scary once you get to know her,' Sophie said.

The three of them walked back to *The Ark*.

'I'll just drop in on your grandad, see how Pat's doing,' said Terry, 'but shall we meet at the same time tomorrow?'

Tom and Sophie smiled and nodded.

'Operation Find Pat's Mum,' said Terry. 'End of Day One.'

Chapter 8

Tom and Sophie went out with Terry for the next six evenings. On the second evening, they accepted that there were no more Daubenton's living on the canal, and after that Terry took them to search further afield. They explored nearby parks and nature reserves and city farms. They talked to vicars and explored church attics; they spoke with caretakers and searched through school lofts.

Everybody seemed keen to help them once they understood the nature of the mission.

Sometimes Tom and Sophie used the bat detector; sometimes they could identify the bats by their call or their size or the shape they made when they flew.

On the sixth evening, Terry bent over and examined some bat droppings in a graveyard. 'Want to learn how to analyse bat poo?' he asked.

Tom looked at Sophie and shrugged. Sophie shrugged back.

'OK,' they both said.

'You can tell a lot about bats from their poo,' Terry said, moving the droppings around with a long plastic stick, 'because all bats have slightly different diets. For example, long-eared bats live in woodlands so they tend to eat more beetles and crickets. Daubenton's like Pat live near water so they eat more moths and midges. You'll often see the remains of these insects in their poo.'

'There's some poo over here,' Tom said, crouching down and pushing a brown lump with a stick, 'but I can't see any insects in it.'

Terry glanced up. 'That's because it's a dog poo, Tom.'

'Oh, OK, right,' Tom said, standing up quickly. 'Thought it looked familiar.'

'Each bat species also has different-shaped poo,' said Terry. 'Pipistrelle poo is just tiny dots. A Daubenton's is twice as long and sort of curvy.'

'So we need to look for curvy poo with midges in it,' Sophie said.

'Yep,' agreed Terry.

He got down on his hands and knees and put his face right up against a few greyish streaks on a gravestone. He sniffed and put his little finger in it.

Tom knelt down beside Terry. Then Sophie sighed and knelt down next to Tom.

'Hey, Soph,' Tom said. 'I'll be in charge of this assignment. But you can be my number two if you like. Geddit? My number two!'

Sophie glared at Tom, and Tom stopped smiling.

At the end of the evening, after they had explored every tree and every poo in the Camley Street Nature Park, Terry sighed and wiped his forehead. 'We're running out of places to look.'

'Are you saying we should give up?' Sophie asked.

'Not give up, but we might have to think about a plan B,' Terry replied.

'You mean, we look after Pat ourselves?' Tom asked. 'Like we originally planned?'

'Maybe,' Terry said.

'But I thought you said she really needed to be with other bats,' said Sophie.

'I did,' said Terry. 'She does. Look, let's have a night off tomorrow and see what we think about everything on Sunday.'

When they got back to the marina that night, Tom and Sophie headed for Grandad's boat. They went into the darkroom and looked at Pat scuttling backwards and forward in her box. They both took turns feeding her milk and mealworms.

'It's great looking after her,' said Sophie, 'but what happens when she starts flying?'

'And she might want to get married and have kids,' said Tom. 'Who's she going to marry stuck in here? Grandad?'

Sophie chuckled. 'We can't give up yet, can we, Tom?' she said.

Tom shook his head. 'Not until we've completed our mission.'

On Saturday Tom and Sophie headed to the zoo with their parents.

'What are you going to look at today, kids?' Mr Nightingale asked, as they went through the staff turnstile. 'Let me guess – bats?'

'Not *just* bats,' said Tom.

They headed for the Nightzone and, after a brief look at the potto and a quick glimpse at the armadillo, they stood in front of the Seba's Short-tailed Bats.

'You can tell they're not meant to live alone, can't you?' said Sophie, as she watched the bats flitting from one part of the enclosure to another and huddling together in small groups.

Tom nodded. 'A bat needs its friends and family.'

They watched the bats for another couple of minutes.

Then Tom noticed two boxes fixed to the back wall of the enclosure.

'Hey, look, they've got a house back there,' said Tom.

Sophie smiled. 'I wonder what's inside.'

'And I wonder how you make one,' murmured

Tom. His eyes suddenly widened. 'Soph, that's it!'

'What's it?' Sophie said.

'We'll build Pat's mum a house. Then she'll definitely come back.'

'What? Where?'

'Exactly where we first saw her. By the bridge near *The Ark*.'

'That's actually a good idea,' said Sophie. 'It'll mean that, if Pat's mum is flying past, or her colony changes roost again, they might see a bat box and snuggle in there.'

'Exactly!' said Tom. 'Come on.'

'Where are we going?' Sophie asked, as Tom dragged her out of the Nightzone.

'To find Dad of course,' Tom said. 'He can build anything.'

They ran to the large-mammal section, where their father worked. They found him walking across the green towards Gorilla Kingdom, carrying a bucket full of chopped-up vegetables.

Tom told him about their plan.

'A bat box, eh?' Mr Nightingale said. 'Well you're in luck. I built the one in the Nightzone. I think I still remember how I did it.'

He pulled a notepad out of his top pocket and started scribbling on it.

'This is what we'll need,' said Mr Nightingale. 'Give this list to Grandad. He can take you to the DIY shop.'

Tom, Sophie and Grandad returned from the local DIY shop with armfuls of wood, pencils and nails — plus a small saw and a bottle of special glue.

Mr Nightingale was already at Grandad's barge. He'd drawn a sketch of the bat box — a rectangular shape, about thirty centimetres high, with a narrow slot in the bottom that the bats could crawl through. There would be a ladder on the back wall of the box. About thirty Daubenton's bats would be able to fit inside.

Dad put everyone to work. Sophie helped to measure everything, placing the ruler on the wood and drawing marks around the edges with a pencil. Grandad and Tom made the ladder, with Grandad sawing the wood for the rungs and Tom gluing the sides together.

Soon the bat box was complete.

'Do we need to put varnish or anything on it?' Sophie asked. 'To stop the rain getting in?'

'No, it's perfect as it is,' Mr Nightingale said. 'We won't treat the wood at all. It needs to be rough and knobbly. So bats can cling on to the outside and the inside.'

Ten minutes later, Terry appeared.

'Your grandad phoned,' he said. 'Apparently you've got something to show me. This must be it.' He nodded at the brand new, home-made bat box on the table. 'Did you make that?' he asked, picking it up gently.

Tom and Sophie nodded.

'That is a masterpiece,' Terry said, turning it from side to side.

'I thought we could put it near the bridge,' Tom said. 'Maybe Pat's mum will see it and move in.'

Terry smiled. 'That's a great idea. It's about a week since they shifted roost. The weather's got much warmer, so they could well return to their original home – down here where it's cooler.' He examined the bat box again. 'This is a palace. What bat wouldn't want to live in this?'

Tom, Sophie and Terry were soon sprinting along the towpath. Sophie was holding the bat box, Tom had the toolbox and Terry was carrying a stepladder.

When they reached the bridge, Terry said, 'OK, where shall we put our box?'

'Up there?' suggested Tom, pointing to a nearby tree.

'It's not very sheltered,' said Terry. 'Bats prefer to be out of the way.'

'Over there?' suggested Tom, indicating a smaller tree by the bridge wall.

'It's quite far from the water,' said Terry. 'Let's try to get closer to the canal.'

'How about there?' Sophie suggested, pointing to a tree that arched over the water. 'It's near the canal, and look – it's got flowers growing under it! They'll attract butterflies and moths.'

'Well spotted, Sophie,' said Terry.

'That's quite a good idea, I suppose,' said Tom grudgingly.

Terry leant the ladder against the tree, wedging the top end under a branch. Then he started to climb up. When he got to the top, Sophie climbed up the first couple of rungs and handed him the box.

'Hammer and nails,' said Terry.

Tom scrambled halfway up the ladder and passed Terry the tools.

After a minute or two, Terry said, 'I can't seem to hold the box still and hammer in a nail at the same time.'

Tom and Sophie looked at each other.

'Why didn't you say?' Sophie said.

Both Tom and Sophie leapt on to the lowest branch of the tree and pulled themselves up to the next branch and then the next and the next. In a few seconds, they were eye to eye with Terry.

'We're pretty good at climbing trees,' Sophie said.

Terry smiled. 'Very handy. Tom, you hold the bottom of the box. Sophie, you hold the top.'

Tom moved around to the other side of the tree. Then both Tom and Sophie leant forward, each putting one arm around the tree trunk and the other on the bat box, holding it in place while Terry gently tapped nails into the bottom and sides.

'Done,' said Terry.

He started to climb down the ladder.

When he reached the ground, he was startled to see Tom and Sophie standing on the towpath, waiting for him.

'We're good at climbing down trees too,' Sophie explained.

Tom glanced up at the bat box. 'So what happens now?'

'Well, it depends,' Terry said. 'There's no point us staying here. The bats won't arrive till it's dark. Truth is, the best thing we could do is . . . build another box!'

'Really?' Tom said.

Terry nodded.

'Cool!' Tom exclaimed.

'Did you have much wood left?' Terry asked.

'Loads,' said Sophie.

'The more boxes we can put up there,' Terry said, 'the more chance we have of attracting Pat's mum. We should put up maybe three or four, at different heights and facing different directions.'

Tom, Sophie, Terry, Grandad and Mr Nightingale built another two boxes that evening. Terry, Tom and Sophie managed to fix them both to the same tree trunk before it became too dark to see.

'OK,' Terry said, climbing down the ladder. 'Now let's get out of here. We don't want to scare any bats off.'

Tom, Sophie and Terry walked down the towpath and stood next to a bush at least thirty metres away.

Terry turned his bat detector on. It was dusk and the outline of the tree with its bat boxes sticking out was visible in the distance.

Tom and Sophie had brought their special torches. They switched them on and two reddish beams shot through the grey evening light.

Half an hour passed. Nothing happened.

Then Terry's bat detector made a scuffling, shuffling sound.

'Daubenton's,' whispered Tom and Sophie.

A few bats gathered by the bridge. They swooped down towards the canal, skimmed across the surface of the water and took off again.

'I think that one caught three midges at once,' Tom said, training his beam on the third bat as it vanished into the sky.

More bats gathered. They also tracked across the water, scooping up insects with their claws and pouches.

Sophie shone her torch on the lowest bat box and then on the other two.

'They're ignoring the boxes,' she said with a sigh.

'Give them a chance,' said Terry.

'There! Look!' Tom whispered. He was holding the beam of his torch on the lowest box.

A bat was scuttling up the ladder and sniffing at the bottom of the box.

'Go on, go on, go on,' urged Terry.

But the bat pushed itself off and disappeared into the night.

'I don't believe it,' said Sophie.

Over the course of the evening, a couple more bats inspected the bat boxes but neither ventured inside.

'We'll come back tomorrow,' Terry said. 'I've got a good feeling about tomorrow.'

'But how much longer do we have,' Sophie asked, 'before Pat's mum forgets who Pat is?'

'Lots of time,' said Terry. But his voice sounded flat and he had a worried expression on his face.

Tom and Sophie followed Terry back to *The Ark*, feeling frustrated.

'We'll just have to build more boxes,' said Tom, 'and put them on every tree on the canal. Until there's nowhere else for the bats to land. That's GOT to work.'

Sophie nodded slowly, trying to hide her gloominess.

'Let's go and give Pat her dinner,' she said.

Chapter 9

The next evening, Tom and Sophie went to Grandad's houseboat as usual. They were surprised to see that Terry was already there. Pat's box was also on the kitchen table.

'What's Pat doing out of the darkroom?' Sophie asked. 'It's not time for her to go to sleep yet.'

'It's only temporary,' said Grandad. 'Terry has some exciting news.'

'Pat's going to come with us tonight,' Terry said.

'Cool. How come?' Tom asked.

'Because there are *lots* of bats in the area,' Terry said, 'really close to our bat boxes.'

'Brilliant!' Tom exclaimed.

'And are they . . . ?' Sophie stammered. 'I mean, could they be . . . ?'

'They're Daubenton's,' Terry said. 'Of course, Pat's mum might not be one of them. And even if she is, the bats might not roost in our boxes. But still . . .'

Sophie smiled. 'Let's go.'

'I'm coming with you!' Grandad declared. 'This I've got to see!'

Grandad and Terry packed everything they needed into a bag: gloves, torches, Pat's food, the bat detector and Grandad's old-fashioned camera.

Finally, they picked up Pat's box from the kitchen table.

'How's she looking?' Terry said, peering in.

'She's fine,' said Sophie, smiling down into the box.

Pat was peering up at Terry and Sophie, digging her wings into the bottom of the box and lifting herself up and along.

Five minutes later, the four of them were striding along the towpath. They stopped about twenty metres away from the bat boxes. It was starting to get dark, but no bats were visible in the sky.

'How do you know they're around there?' Tom asked.

Terry shone his torch at a pile of droppings at the bottom of the tree.

'Did you analyse them already?' Tom asked.

'They're Daubenton's all right,' said Terry. 'Full of moths.'

'And midges?' asked Tom.

'And midges,' confirmed Terry.

Half an hour later, just after sunset, a group of bats started to swirl around the tree with all the bat boxes on. A few seconds later, even more bats joined them.

Terry handed the bat detector to Sophie, who tuned it in.

She nodded. 'Daubenton's.'

Now there were lots of bats, maybe a hundred, maybe more.

They broke off into smaller groups, some hovering over the canal, some ducking under the bridge, others continuing to glide between the trees. The bat detector was going crazy – it was already a blizzard of thuds and clicks.

Tom and Sophie looked up and around – spellbound.

'I've never seen so many bats in one place,' Sophie whispered.

'Let's just hope they're here to stay,' murmured Terry, 'and that Pat's mum is one of them.'

Grandad pointed his stick at the middle bat box. 'There! And there!'

A Daubenton's bat was climbing into the box that faced the canal. Another was crawling into the bat box lower down the tree.

'They're roosting,' Terry whispered excitedly. He turned to Tom and Sophie.

'Ready for this?'

'Ready for what?' Tom replied.

'We have to put Pat below the bat boxes,' said Terry.

Terry put on his gloves.

Tom and Sophie looked at each other. Until now, they hadn't fully realised what was about to happen. They both started to talk at the same time, then both stopped. Finally Sophie said, 'Hang on — are we sure she's strong enough?'

'Yeah,' Tom added. 'Has she had enough milk today?'

'Maybe we should wait,' said Sophie. 'I'm sure her wing hasn't completely healed.'

Terry looked at Tom and Sophie with a smile. He put one arm around Tom's shoulder and one around Sophie.

'It's been quite a mission, hasn't it?' he said.

Tom and Sophie nodded.

'She's a pretty incredible bat,' he added.

Tom and Sophie nodded again.

He took the gloves off and held them out.

'I think you should do this,' he said.

Tom and Sophie looked at each other. They thought for a few seconds.

'She does belong with her mother,' said Sophie.

Tom sighed and nodded. 'And if we do it, she won't be scared,' he said. 'She does know us really well.'

Sophie nodded. 'I'll carry the box. You handle her.'

The two of them walked slowly and quietly towards the tree. Sophie put down the box as gently as she could.

Tom put the gloves on and lifted Pat carefully out of the box, placing her carefully on a soft clump of moss. Pat wriggled slightly, turning herself around with her wings.

Tom stroked her gently with a gloved finger and then stepped back. Both children stared at Pat for a few seconds; she was still so tiny, so helpless.

'We're doing the right thing, aren't we?' Sophie whispered.

'I thought you knew,' said Tom.

Sophie bit her lip. 'We're doing the right thing,' she said.

They walked away. Sophie was holding the empty box. Tom was carrying Terry's gloves.

They returned to where Terry and Grandad were standing. Grandad was snapping away with his camera. Terry was tuning in his bat detector so he could listen to the Daubenton's bats skimming across the canal.

Tom and Sophie crouched down and both trained their torches on the patch of grass where Pat was lying. They could just about make her out: a small brown smudge on an even darker lump.

Then Tom had a thought.

'Can I borrow your camera, Grandad?' Tom asked.

'Of course!' exclaimed Grandad, handing it over to his grandson.

Tom held up the camera to his eye and pressed the zoom button, magnifying Pat twenty times. He was careful not to wobble the camera too much, as every time he did, he lost where Pat was and had to zoom out and locate her with the viewfinder again.

'Is she still there?' Sophie asked.

Tom nodded.

Grandad put a hand on Tom's shoulder. 'What's that up there?' he asked. 'Can you zoom in on it, Tom?'

Tom pointed the camera upwards and zoomed in.

Terry squinted. 'Blast, it looks like an owl.'

Tom squinted through the viewfinder. 'It is an owl,' he said.

'Describe it,' Terry said.

'I can only just make it out in this light,' said Tom. 'Round face. Reddish brown feathers. Whiter feathers on its chest.'

'Damn it,' said Terry, 'it's a tawny owl.'

'Why's that so bad?' asked Tom.

'Because tawny owls eat bats, you dimwit,' said Sophie. 'Especially baby bats. We've got to get Pat out of there.'

'Hang on, hang on,' said Grandad, holding her back.

'Let go, Grandad,' said Sophie. 'I'm not letting Pat get eaten.'

'Look, the owl's just circling at the moment,' said Grandad, 'and think about how owls hunt. They listen and they look. Now, Pat's not making any noise. Not compared to all the mice and rats that are scurrying along the canal this evening. And she's not moving either. Just sitting there on her patch of moss.'

'Sorry, Grandad, it's too dangerous,' Sophie said, stepping forward.

'Sophie,' Grandad said, 'I know it's hard to say goodbye to Pat. But she doesn't belong with you and me. She belongs out there.'

Sophie looked up at him.

'Give her a chance,' said Grandad. 'Let's see how she does in the big wide world.'

He squeezed Sophie's shoulder and she nodded.

'Keep the camera trained on that owl,' said Terry. 'Your grandad's right. He's unlikely to swoop, but let's not take any chances.'

Tom continued to point the camera up at the sky.

Grandad and Sophie watched more Daubenton's circling the tree and crawling into the bat boxes.

'Do you think one of them is Pat's mum?' asked Sophie.

'Well, those bats knew that this was a good place for a roost,' said Grandad. 'Chances are they've been around here before.'

Sophie glanced up at the sky again. 'I still don't trust that owl,' she murmured.

Then Tom said, 'Did you hear that?'

'Hear what?' Terry and Grandad said.

'It's that fox again,' Tom said. 'I recognise its growl.'

They all listened. 'I hear it too,' Sophie said.

'OK, Grandad, it's officially too dangerous. We have to get Pat.'

'It does feel a bit dangerous out there,' Terry said.

'All of you need to calm down,' said Grandad with a smile. 'When you're as old as me, you'll realise that animals in the wild are surrounded by predators twenty-four hours a day, seven days a week. And, believe it or not, most of them make it through to bedtime.'

'But Pat can't even fly away,' said Tom.

They heard a scuffling behind them.

'It's the fox, it must be,' said Sophie.

'Just wait a second,' said Grandad, 'please.'

Tom peered through the camera again. 'The owl's gone.'

He paused and squinted again. 'Oh no, he hasn't. He's seen something.'

'Grandad, PLEASE let me get Pat,' Sophie begged.

'She's fine,' Grandad said, 'and she'll go on being fine.'

Sophie was looking up at the sky and around at the undergrowth. She was convinced that the fox, the owl or maybe even a stray dog was on its way to swallow Pat whole.

'Look,' whispered Grandad.

A bat had landed right next to Pat. They all shone their torches at the two bats. The combined light from all four torches made the grass glow red. Pat was twisting around to face the adult bat, who was manoeuvring itself next to her. Pat lifted up her tiny wings and flung herself on top of the adult bat. She fidgeted sideways, gripping with her wings.

Then the adult bat flew off, with the tiny figure of Pat holding tightly on to her back.

'Pat . . . Pat's mum,' Tom stammered.

Sophie couldn't move or speak. She just stared at the brown shape as it circled one of the bat boxes.

'They found each other,' said Terry. 'I don't believe it.'

'And you know what the best thing is?' Grandad said. 'She hasn't gone far.'

He nodded at the lowest bat box. Pat's mum was clinging to the bottom, dragging herself inside.

'You can come and see her whenever you want.'

Sophie gave a sob of relief and delight.

Tom handed Grandad the camera and said, 'Owls are amazing, aren't they? Let's get into owls next!'

Chapter 10

The following morning, Tom and Sophie felt both happy and sad. Happy that Pat had found her mum; sad that Pat didn't live on Grandad's boat any more.

They had got used to the routine of feeding Pat her milk and mealworms during the day and then bat-watching on Regent's Canal at night.

'It won't be the same,' said Tom, as he sat at the breakfast table and munched his cornflakes, 'visiting Pat in a bat box.'

Sophie nodded. 'Most of the time we won't even be able to see her.'

They went to their rooms and got ready for school. When they came back into the kitchen, Terry was waiting for them, chatting to their mum and dad.

'I've got good news and bad news,' he said. 'Which do you want first?'

'Bad news,' said Tom.

'Good news,' said Sophie.

'Bad news, you dummy,' said Tom. 'Then the good news is a nice surprise.'

'No, good news first,' said Sophie. 'Then the bad news doesn't seem so bad.'

'Well, it's all good news really,' said Terry. 'First of all, Pat's settled in nicely. No sign of her being rejected. She's fitted in with all her aunts, uncles and cousins.'

'That is good news, I suppose,' said Sophie, smiling weakly.

'To be honest, that was the bad news,' said Terry, 'because I know you miss Pat and secretly want to look after her again. The good news is going to make up for all that though.'

Mr and Mrs Nightingale exchanged a glance and smiled.

'The zoo's got to move a group of nocturnal animals up to Whipsnade Zoo,' said Terry.

'Oh,' said Tom.

'We need to make sure they're in safe hands,' said Terry. 'You know, PROPER experts.'

'OK,' said Sophie.

'Usually we move nocturnal animals during the day,' Terry said, 'take them out of the Nightzone – which confuses them a bit, as they're used to day being night and night being day. It would be nice if we could move them into a similar environment. Somewhere artificially dark.'

Sophie had twigged and started to grin.

'So we were looking around for some kind of darkroom,' said Terry, 'and for a group of people – you know, maybe a keeper, a vet and two young helpers – who might be able to escort the animals to Whipsnade.'

Tom had cottoned on too and was also grinning.

'We need to move an armadillo, a jumping rat and a slender loris,' said Terry, 'but what's the best way of getting them to Whipsnade?'

'Grandad's barge!' Tom and Sophie exclaimed together.

Mrs Nightingale said, 'We thought we could sail up this weekend. It's a bank holiday so you don't have to be in school till Tuesday.'

'You'll need to check them over every morning,' Terry said, 'give them their breakfast, change their bedding. Help your mum if they get sick. Help your dad with any training they need. Think you can manage it?'

Tom and Sophie were too excited to speak, but they nodded very quickly.

'Excellent,' said Terry. 'I'll bring the animals around on Friday.'

He said goodbye and walked off *The Ark*, leaving Tom and Sophie gobsmacked.

Mr and Mrs Nightingale waited for the children to talk or move but nothing happened.

'Maybe they're both bats,' said Mr Nightingale. 'You know, they're making noises but they're too high-pitched for us to hear.'

Then Tom and Sophie started to squeak with delight.

'Definitely bats,' said Mrs Nightingale with a smile. 'Totally bats.'

More amazing behind-the-scenes animal action
at London Zoo
with the Nightingale family!

Stop! There's a Snake in Your Suitcase!
by Adam Frost

What's that slithering by the canal? Uh-oh.
There's a mysterious case of smuggled snakes.
It's Tom and Sophie to the rescue!

OUT NOW

More amazing behind-the-scenes animal action
at London Zoo
with the Nightingale family!

Run! The Elephant Weighs a Ton!
by Adam Frost

The animal-mad Nightingale family are charging out
of town towards a jumbo-sized mystery. Their animal
friends need them. Whoa! What a fright for the new baby
elephant. Something just isn't right. It's up to Tom and
Sophie to find out what!

OUT NOW

Don't miss exciting adventures
in the realm of the Amur tiger in

Paw Prints in the Snow
by Sally Grindley

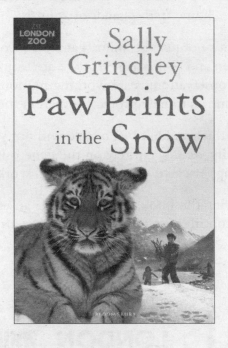

Joe and his family are in Russia on the trail of one of the
world's rarest creatures, the beautiful Amur tiger.

Exploring a vast, freezing nature reserve, Joe comes closer
to the tigers than he ever imagined – and is drawn into a
daring mission to rescue an injured cub . . .

OUT NOW

Zoological Society of London

ZSL London Zoo is a very famous part of the Zoological Society of London (ZSL).

For almost two hundred years, we have been working tirelessly to provide hope and a home to thousands of animals.

And it's not just the animals at ZSL's Zoos in London and Whipsnade that we are caring for. Our conservationists are working in more than 50 countries to help protect animals in the wild.

But all of this wouldn't be possible without your help. As a charity we rely entirely on the generosity of our supporters to continue this vital work.

By buying this book, you have made an essential contribution to help protect animals.
Thank you.

Find out more at **zsl.org**

ZSL
LIVING CONSERVATION

ZSL
LONDON
ZOO

ZSL
WHIPSNADE
ZOO